He Shall Arise

AN EASTER WORK FOR CHOIR, SOLOISTS
AND INSTRUMENTS

by TOM FETTKE

ORCHESTRATIONS BY
DON MARSH

The creator of "He Shall Arise" wishes to thank Bill Wolaver,
Robin Wolaver and Don Marsh for their significant
contributions to this Easter work.

COMPANION PRODUCTS:
Choral Book 0-7673-9894-7
Listening CD 0-7673-9932-3
Listening Cassette 0-7673-9941-2
Accompaniment CD 0-7673-9933-1 (Split-track only)
Accompaniment Cassette 0-7673-9959-5 (Side A Split-track; Side B Instruments only)
Rehearsal Tracks 0-7673-9927-7
Orchestration 0-7673-9953-6
CD Promo Pak 0-7673-9967-6
Cassette Promo Pak 0-7673-9975-7

Instrumentation includes: Flute 1-2, Oboe, Clarinet 1-2, Bassoon, Trumpet 1-2-3, French Horn 1-2, Trombone 1-2-3, Tuba, Percussion, Timpani, Harp, Piano, Violin, Viola, Cello, String Bass
Substitute Parts: Alto Sax 1-2 (substitute for French Horn 1-2), Tenor Sax/Baritone Treble Clef (substitute for Trombone 1-2), Clarinet 3 (substitute for Viola), Bass Clarinet (substitute for Bassoon), Keyboard String Reduction

GENEVOX

© Copyright 1998 GENEVOX (a div. of GMG), Nashville, TN 37234.

He Shall Arise
by Tom Fettke

Foreword

Tom Fettke has effectively captured, through music, the emotion of the death, burial, and resurrection of Jesus Christ in *He Shall Arise*. His dramatic use of classical choral literature is tastefully surrounded by compositions from today's most sensitive writers, reminding us of the pain and agony Jesus suffered on the cross, as well as the victory of the Resurrection.

Your heart will sense the despair of the disciples when Jesus was arrested in the Garden as they "forsook him, and fled"(Matt. 26:56). Tom Fettke has also captured the dramatic change in the lives of the disciples from fear to unlimited courage as they went everywhere telling the news of the Resurrection (Acts 8: 1-4).

The death of Jesus Christ is mentioned more than 120 times in the New Testament and is spoken of many times by the prophets in the Old Testament. In John 10: 17-18, Jesus said, "No man taketh it [life] from me, but I lay it down of myself." He also said, " I have power to take it [up] again." The Resurrection fulfills prophecy and the claims of Jesus. *He Shall Arise* reminds us of the biblical truths of the gospel. Because of the Resurrection, every Sunday for the believer should be Easter! *Hallelujah, to God's Almighty Son!*

ROBERT R. WAGONER
Large Church/Worship Consultant
Music Ministries Department
LifeWay Christian Resources
of the Southern Baptist Convention

Contents

PART I - HE SHALL ARISE 7
OVERTURE AND OPENING
includes
Excerpts from FINLANDIA/WERE YOU THERE/HE SHALL ARISE

PART II - THE TRIUMPHAL ENTRY 20
includes
HOSANNA! *from the* HOLY CITY/RIDE ON, KING JESUS

PART III - THE LAST SUPPER 31
includes
AT THE END OF THE WEEK/COMMUNION SONG

PART IV - GETHSEMANE 38
includes
'TIS MIDNIGHT, AND ON OLIVE'S BROW/ALONE IN GETHSEMANE

PART V - THE ARREST AND TRIAL 46
includes
LET HIM BE CRUCIFIED

PART VI - THE CRUCIFIXION 54
includes
CROSS OF JESUS, CROSS OF SORROW/INTO YOUR HANDS/
SURELY HE HATH BORNE OUR GRIEFS

PART VII - THE RESURRECTION 68
includes
HE SHALL ARISE/THE VICTOR/I AM THE LIVING ONE

PART VIII - THE PROMISE 86
includes
HALLELUJAH *from* MOUNT OF OLIVES/THOU THE PROMISE

Part I
HE SHALL ARISE

Overture and Opening
includes
Excerpts from *Finlandia*
Were You There
He Shall Arise

*Arranged by Tom Fettke
and Don Marsh*

Sw. Flutes 8' and 4', Principal 4'
Gt. Principals 8' and 4'
Ped. 16' and 8'

*Music by Jean Sibelius
© Copyright 1998 Van Ness Press, Inc. (ASCAP) Distributed by GENEVOX (a div. of GMG). Nashville, TN 37234.

**This part may be played by organ, a second accoustic piano, or synthesizer.

*"Were You There?"

‡Play melody only in absence of organ.

*Traditional Spiritual.

© Copyright 1998 Van Ness Press, Inc. (ASCAP) Distributed by GENEVOX (a div. of GMG). Nashville, TN 37234.

*Music by Jean Sibelius
© Copyright 1998 Van Ness Press, Inc. (ASCAP)Distributed by GENEVOX (a div. of GMG). Nashville, TN 37234.

*Traditional Spiritual.
© Copyright 1998 Van Ness Press, Inc. (ASCAP) Distributed by GENEVOX (a div. of GMG). Nashville, TN 37234.

*Lyrics by Robin Wolaver; Music by Jean Sibelius.
© Copyright 1998 Van Ness Press, Inc. (ASCAP) Distributed by GENEVOX (a div. of GMG). Nashville, TN 37234.

Part II
THE TRIUMPHAL ENTRY
includes
Hosanna! from the *Holy City*
Ride on, King Jesus

Arranged by Tom Fettke

*Lyrics by F.E. Weatherly; Music by Stephen Adams.
© Copyright 1998 Van Ness Press, Inc. (ASCAP) Distributed by GENEVOX (a div. of GMG). Nashville, TN 37234.

*Lyrics by Lorie Marsh, Tom Fettke, and Traditional; Music: Traditional Spiritual.
© Copyright 1998 Van Ness Press, Inc. (ASCAP) Distributed by GENEVOX (a div. of GMG). Nashville, TN 37234.

Part III
THE LAST SUPPER
includes
At the End of the Week
Communion Song

Arranged by Tom Fettke

* Lyrics and Music by Tom Fettke.
© Copyright 1998 Van Ness Press, Inc. (ASCAP) Distributed by GENEVOX (a div. of GMG). Nashville, TN 37234.

** Lyrics and Music by Barry McGuire.
© Copyright 1977 Sparrow Song/Careers BMG Music/Shaunda Music (BMI).
Print rights administeed by EMI Christian Music Publishing.

Part IV
GETHSEMANE
includes
'Tis Midnight, and on Olive's Brow
Alone in Gethsemane

Arranged by Tom Fettke

* Lyrics by William B. Tappan; Music by William B. Bradbury.
© Copyright 1998 Van Ness Press, Inc. (ASCAP) Distributed by GENEVOX (a div. of GMG). Nashville, TN 37234.

40

* Lyrics by Robin Wolaver; Music by Bill Wolaver and Antonio Vivaldi.
© Copyright 1998 Van Ness Press, Inc. (ASCAP) Distributed by GENEVOX (a div. of GMG). Nashville, TN 37234.

*Refrain adapted from Antonio Vivaldi's *Cello Sonata No. 5*

Part V
THE ARREST AND TRIAL
includes
Let Him Be Crucifed

Arranged by Tom Fettke

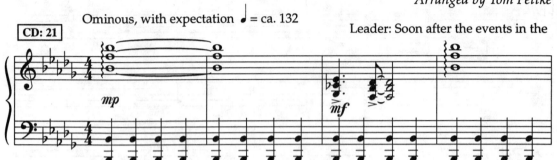

© Copyright 1998 Van Ness Press, Inc. (ASCAP) Distributed by GENEVOX (a div. of GMG). Nashville, TN 37234.

* Lyrics by Robin Wolaver; Music by Bill Wolaver.
© Copyright 1998 Van Ness Press, Inc. (ASCAP) Distributed by GENEVOX (a div. of GMG). Nashville, TN 37234.

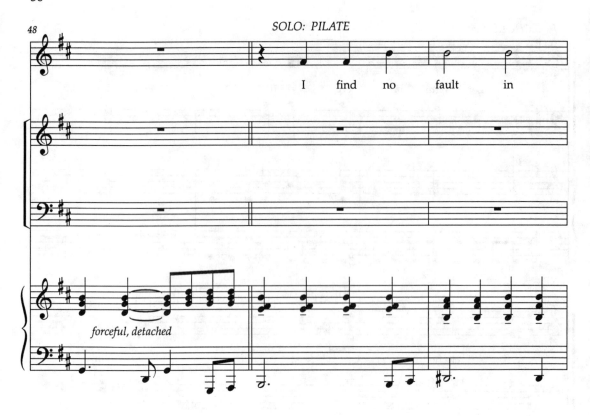

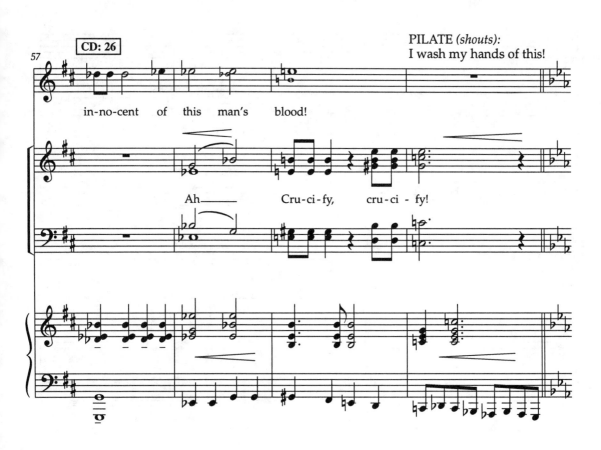

*See next page for further instructions.

Part VI
THE CRUCIFIXION
includes
Cross of Jesus, Cross of Sorrow
Into Your Hands
Surely He Hath Borne Our Griefs

Arranged by Tom Fettke

Hammer Hits *(Five hits occur before underscore begins.)*

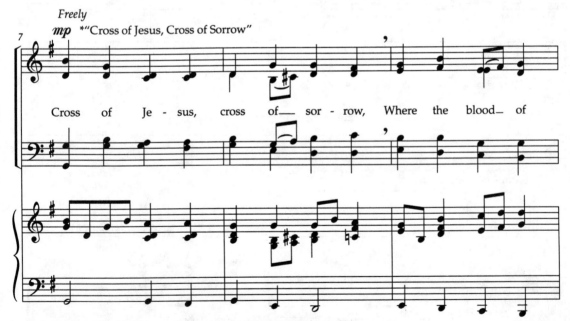

*Lyrics by William J. Sparrow-Simpson; Music by John Stainer.
© Copyright 1998 Van Ness Press, Inc. (ASCAP) Distributed by GENEVOX (a div. of GMG). Nashville, TN 37234.

The hammer hits heard on the recording of "He Shall Arise" are included at the appropriate moment on the accompaniment tracks. For use with live accompaniment, recorded hammer hits are provided at the end of Accompaniment CD (0-7673-9933-1) and at the end of Side B of Accompaniment Cassette (0-7673-9959-5).

*Lyrics and Music by Karen Voegtlin.
© Copyright 1984 Bud John Songs, Inc. (ASCAP) All rights administered by EMI Christian Music Publishing.

*Lyrics adapted from Isaiah 53:4,5; Music by George Frederick Handel.
© Copyright 1998 Van Ness Press, Inc. (ASCAP)Distributed by GENEVOX (a div. of GMG). Nashville, TN 37234.

Part VII
THE RESURRECTION
includes
He Shall Arise
The Victor
I Am the Living One

Arranged by Tom Fettke

* Lyrics by Robin Wolaver; Music by Jean Sibelius
© Copyright 1998 Van Ness Press, Inc. (ASCAP) Distributed by GENEVOX (a div. of GMG). Nashville, TN 37234.

* Lyrics and Music by Jamie Owens-Collins.
© Copyright 1976 Bud John Songs, Inc. (ASCAP) All rights administered by EMI Christian Music Publishing.

* Lyrics by Robin Wolaver; Music by Bill Wolaver
© Copyright 1998 Van Ness Press, Inc. (ASCAP) Distributed by GENEVOX (a div. of GMG). Nashville, TN 37234.

* Lyrics and Music by Jamie Owens-Collins.
© Copyright 1976 Bud John Songs, Inc. (ASCAP) All rights administered by EMI Christian Music Publishing.

* Lyrics by Robin Wolaver; Music by Bill Wolaver
© Copyright 1998 Van Ness Press, Inc. (ASCAP) Distributed by GENEVOX (a div. of GMG). Nashville, TN 37234.

* Lyrics and Music by Jamie Owens-Collins.
© Copyright 1976 Bud John Songs, Inc. (ASCAP) All rights administered by EMI Christian Music Publishing.

Part VIII
THE PROMISE
includes
Hallelujah from *Mount of Olives*
Thou the Promise

Arranged by Tom Fettke

*Lyrics and Music by Ludwig van Beethoven.
© Copyright 1998 Van Ness Press, Inc. (ASCAP) Distributed by GENEVOX (a div. of GMG). Nashville, TN 37234.

*Lyrics by Michael Card; Music by Scott Brasher.
© Copyright 1991 Birdwing Music/MoleEnd Music (ASCAP).
All rights administered by EMI Christian Music Publishing.